A Christmas Journey

SUSIE POOLE

Thanks to Jonnie B, Malcolm Down, Phil Grundy, Julie Clayden, Jo Poole, Peter and Veronica Batsford, John Nicholson and Mum

Text and illustrations copyright ©2014 Susie Poole
Published in 2014 by B&H Publishing Group,
Nashville, Tennessee
Published in association with the literary agency of Hosung Maeng,
Seoul, Republic of Korea
All rights reserved.

Dewey Decimal Classification: C232.92
Subject Heading: JESUS CHRIST—NATIVITY \
CHRISTMAS \ JESUS CHRIST—HUMANITY

ISBN: 978-1-4336-8343-5
Printed in China

1 2 3 4 5   18 17 16 15 14

A Christmas Journey

SUSIE POOLE

Nashville, Tennessee

What an exciting time of year! We're getting ready for Christmas.

The streets look so beautiful as they sparkle with colored lights. Soon our Christmas tree will glow cheerily through the window, heavy with ornaments, ribbons and tinsel.

At home, we light pretty candles and put them on a high shelf where they light up the whole room. As the flames dance this way and that, we remember the time, long ago, when God sent His Christmas light into the world. God loves light. He always has. It was the first thing He had ever made, and it was very, very good.

Here our Christmas journey begins.

When everything was dark, empty and cold, God decided that the time had come to create a beautiful world, full of His wonderful light. So He used His magnificent voice and for the first time ever spoke the words, "Let there be light."

And there was.

God pushed the light and dark apart and in doing so, made the first day.

Now God had many creation ideas buzzing around in His head, and so He made the sky, the sea, and the islands. Then He filled them up with every kind of living thing, big and small: from the most enormous elephant to the teeny-weeniest turtle.

God had nearly finished making His
beautiful, brand-new world when He said . . .
"Let Us make someone extra special,
someone who will be a lot like Us."

"Let Us make a person!"

And so He did.

He made a man called Adam. But Adam was lonely,
and it was not good for him to live alone.
So God gave him a lovely woman to
be his wife, called Eve.

God made Eden, a beautiful garden for Adam and
Eve to live in. There they ruled over the animals,
ate delicious food, and, best of all, walked and
talked with their wonderful Daddy, God.

God wanted Adam and Eve to enjoy all that He had made. He also warned them not to eat fruit from the tree in the middle of the garden. If they ate the fruit, they would certainly die.

Among the shadows lurked a crafty snake who hated God. One day, as Adam and Eve were resting, the snake saw his chance to cause some trouble. Slithering down the trunk of the tree, he told the first and biggest lie that has ever been told.

"Did God really say you will die if you eat the fruit from this tree?"

Eve didn't want to have God rule over her, so she plucked a lovely red apple from the tree and took one big, juicy bite. Eve handed it to Adam, and with his first bite, they felt guilty and very sorry for disobeying God.

They knew they had made a big mistake.

Adam and Eve hoped God would not see what they had done. But it was too late. With a sad and heavy heart, God had no choice but to send them away from the garden, forever.

Adam and Eve cried.

God cried too.

Adam and Eve had disobeyed God. Everything had changed. Away from the garden, they felt cold. So God made them clothes from animal skins to keep them warm. He also later would send someone who would solve all the problems that their disobedience caused.

Adam and Eve had lots of children. Soon they filled the whole earth. The people were full of hate and forgot what it was like to have God's wonderful light living inside them. But God still loved them. He had a plan to bring His light back.

God's plan was like a big jigsaw puzzle. As the years passed, He would give little puzzle pieces to men and women who loved Him and longed for His light. He gave one piece to a man called Isaiah. This is what God said to him . . .

"People who are walking in the darkness will see a great light, for a child will be born and he will rule the world, bringing peace, fairness and goodness. . . . He will be called 'God with Us.'"

Many people tried to guess what the puzzle pieces meant. Some put the pieces together in the wrong order. Nobody could agree on what God would do.

Zechariah and Elizabeth were an old couple who spent their lives loving God, longing for His light, and praying for a family. But now they were too old to have a baby.

Zechariah was a priest who served in the temple in Jerusalem. While on special duty one day, a miracle began to grow in the dark temple corners. A bright light shone all around him, and there, in the middle of it, stood a mighty gleaming angel called Gabriel.

"Greetings!" said the angel. "God is going to give you the son you have always longed for. You will call him John, and he will have the job of getting people ready to meet the Savior King."

Zechariah was amazed. Perhaps that is
why he doubted the angel's words.
But asking the angel whether he had
muddled his message was a big mistake.

To prove it was true, the angel took
away Zechariah's voice until the day
the baby was born.

Zechariah and Elizabeth had plenty
to do. They wanted to be ready for
this special baby.

In the village of Nazareth, their young relative, Mary, was making preparations of her own. She was soon to be married to Joseph.

As Mary swept and baked, washed and mended, she sang "thank You" songs to God. She had no idea that God had chosen her for a very special task.

That night, heaven hushed its singing, and the angel Gabriel visited earth once more to bring God's most important message to Mary.

"You are very blessed, and God is with you," whispered Gabriel. "He will surprise you with a Son, and you will call Him Jesus. His Kingdom will rule for ever and ever. The spirit of God will rest on you so that your baby will be called the Son of God."

Gabriel told Mary all about Zechariah and Elizabeth's miracle baby.

"You see," he smiled, "nothing is impossible for God!"

"Yes," replied Mary, "I do see. Let everything you have said happen to me."

Mary quickly packed her things and joined some travelers journeying to Elizabeth's village in Judea.

"Is anybody home?" called Mary. At the sound of these words, the baby in Elizabeth's tummy leapt and wriggled. This baby knew that somebody special had arrived.

Elizabeth was so happy that she laughed, cried, and sang a new song. . . .
"You are so blessed,
More blessed than the rest,
Your baby has caused me to sing.
But who am I that you should come
To me, with such great news to bring?"

Mary sang too . . .

"I'm dancing and singing the song of my God,

I'm happy as happy could be.

Though I'm just a servant with nothing to give,

God chose to give blessings to me.

The weak will be strong,

The poor will be rich,

The proud won't be proud anymore.

He promised to give us this wonderful gift.

Now it's waiting for us at the door."

While the baby was growing in Elizabeth's tummy, Zechariah was unable to speak. So when the baby was born and let out his first cry, Zechariah let out a cry too.

When the time came to name the baby, Zechariah remembered what the angel Gabriel had said and called him John.

"God, You are fantastic," cried Zechariah. "You are giving us one who will show us Your light in the darkness. You have remembered Your promises to us. And my son John has arrived first to make sure that everyone is ready to meet the one who is coming."

It was time to leave. With wonder in her heart, Mary kissed baby John, said goodbye, and began the long journey home.

Now that Mary had returned to Nazareth, it was time to tell Joseph about all the amazing events that had taken place. First she told him about Zechariah and Elizabeth's baby. Joseph thought this was wonderful news, and he clapped with joy. Then Mary told Joseph about her baby.

This, Joseph decided, was not good news. He did not believe that the baby had been put in Mary's tummy by God.

He no longer wanted Mary to be his wife.
Mary was very upset.

That night, an angel visited Joseph in his dreams
and told him that the baby really was God's Son.
Joseph was to call Him Jesus. Joseph was so happy
that he could marry Mary after all.

Many months had passed, and the baby was soon to be born. Mary's tummy was large and sore. Joseph told her that the Roman rulers had ordered everyone to travel to their family town to sign their names in a big book. Mary was not happy because they had to go all the way to Bethlehem.

They packed their clothes, strips of cloths for the baby, and plenty of food and water. God was with them. He smiled on them all the way.

When Mary and Joseph arrived in Bethlehem, it was bustling with visitors. There was no room for Mary except in the place where the animals were kept.

The stable was bustling with all kinds of animal life. The bull in the corner huffed and snorted, tossing his tail this way and that. Little mice scurried and squeaked in and out of an upturned basket.

With Mary comfortable and the donkey fed and watered, Joseph looked around their tatty stable home. Could their baby King really be born in such a humble place?

When Jesus was born, Mary was overjoyed.

She scooped Him up in her arms and marveled at God's amazing miracle. Wrapping Him carefully in strips of cloth, she laid Him in a manger to sleep.

On the hillside outside Bethlehem, a group of shepherds sat around a fire, keeping warm.

That night, as the shepherds' laughter rolled about the hilltop, a strange light grew above them. Soon it was shining all around. When the shepherds saw a mighty angel standing in the night sky, they were terrified.

"Don't be afraid," the angel told them. "I have great news to tell you. A King has been born. He is called Jesus. This is what you should look for—a baby wrapped in strips of cloth, lying in a manger." The sky seemed to explode as a host of angels began swooping and singing, "Glory to God in the highest heaven, and peace on earth to people He favors!"

The light was fading now, and the songs were no more than a whisper. The shepherds helped each other to their feet. They began to stumble, then walk, and then run toward the village.

"God's eyes are on me!" shouted one of the shepherds. "God is with us!" sang another. As they ran, they began to laugh. Joy bubbled inside them like a mountain stream.

They found the stable where Jesus lay, and as they walked through the door they were overwhelmed. There was Jesus, their King. They fell to their knees and worshiped Him. Jesus would give them a new start. He had turned their darkness into light.

It was still night when the shepherds left the stable. But they did not leave quietly. As they sang, Bethlehem woke from its sleep. Leaning out of windows and standing in doorways, people heard the good news about Jesus and shared the shepherds' joy.

A few weeks later, Mary and Joseph took Jesus to visit the temple in Jerusalem.

An old man called Simeon had spent his whole life watching, waiting, and praying for God to send His light back into the world. Today God told Simeon he should visit the temple, for something wonderful would be waiting for him.

As Simeon entered the crowded temple courts, he saw Joseph with a basket containing a gift of two pure white doves and Mary standing close by, holding baby Jesus. As Simeon took the baby and cradled Him in his arms, his heart was bursting with thanks to God.

"Now I have seen with my own eyes the light that will change the world. At last I can die in peace."

Simeon warned Mary and Joseph that Jesus' job was to show people that their lives needed to change and that this would make some of them angry. In fact, just by hearing about His birth, someone was already very angry.

King Herod had no idea about Jesus' birth until a group of travelers called the wise men turned up at the palace. "Where is the baby King?" they asked. "We saw His star in the East and have come to worship Him."

King Herod was proud and evil. He would not allow some baby to be as important as he was. No way! God had spoken about a Savior King being born in Bethlehem. Perhaps this baby was the one.

King Herod pushed the wise men out of the palace door and pointed toward Bethlehem. "Go and search everywhere for the baby," he snarled, "and when you find Him, come back and tell me so that I too can worship Him."

This was untrue of course. What King Herod planned to do was much worse.

The star went ahead of the wise men and came to rest over a scruffy little house on the outskirts of Bethlehem. The wise men looked out of place in their beautiful, rainbow-colored clothes. Still they gladly knelt down and worshiped the baby.

Opening their treasure box, they presented baby Jesus with gifts of gold, frankincense, and myrrh. Each gift was like a story, telling something about who Jesus was and what He would do.

Gold was a costly gift, fit for a king. Jesus the King! What a lovely present.

Frankincense was a sweet-smelling perfume used to worship God.
Jesus was God's Son! How clever of the wise men.

But myrrh? This was a spice used to get people ready for burial!
Did the wise men really want Mary and Joseph to think about Jesus dying?

As the wise men slept that night, they were warned in a dream not to return to Herod's palace. Their lives were in danger, and they must travel home by a secret route.

When Herod realized that the wise men were not coming back to the palace to tell him where Jesus could be found, he was furious. They had tricked him. In his madness he gave orders to kill every boy child in Bethlehem under two years old.

"Get up," said the angel to Joseph in a dream. "Take Jesus and His mother and escape to Egypt. Stay there until I tell you to leave because Herod wants to kill the Child."

Joseph, Mary, and Jesus found safety in Egypt. There they lived, safe in God's hands, until Herod died. Then God's angel appeared to Joseph once more in a dream, saying, "Herod is dead. It's time to go home."

Our Christmas journey has come to an end. Mary and Joseph began life as an ordinary little family, working, eating, and playing. Angels no longer talked to them in their dreams, and strange visitors did not pass by to worship Jesus.

In her heart, Mary remembered all the wonderful things that happened to Jesus and all that was said about Him. There would be many difficult times ahead, but Mary would always remind herself that Jesus was God's gift to the world.

And what a wonderful gift He is. There is so much to be enjoyed at Christmas, but when all the tree lights have been taken down and the parties have ended, Jesus will still be there, showing us God's love and His amazing light.

Thank You, Jesus.

GLOSSARY

ANGEL
A messenger from God

BETHLEHEM
The town where Jesus was born

BLESS
Make someone happy, give them a gift, or help them

CREATION
When God made the world

GABRIEL
An angel sent by God to tell Zechariah and also Mary about having a son

GARDEN OF EDEN
The place God made for Adam and Eve to live in

HEAVEN
God's special place where everything is perfect

IMMANUEL
A name that means "God with Us"

ISAIAH
A man who had a special message from God about Jesus. He told it to people more than 700 years before Jesus was born.

JERUSALEM
The most important city near to where Jesus lived

JOHN	John the Baptist. Zechariah and Elizabeth were his parents.
MANGER	Where hay was put for the animals to eat
MIRACLE	When God does something in an amazing or unexpected way
NAZARETH	The town where Joseph and Mary lived; Jesus lived here until He was about 30 years old.
PRIEST	Someone who helped people worship God
ROMAN RULERS	The rulers of the country where Jesus lived
SAVIOR	Someone who rescues people
SPIRIT OF GOD	The way God works in the world
TEMPLE	A building where people went to worship God
WORSHIP	The way we let God know how much we love Him and say thank You for what He has done